Rock On, Kindness!
Pass It On!

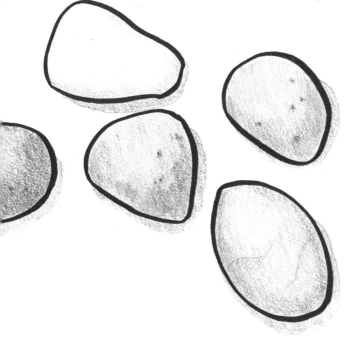

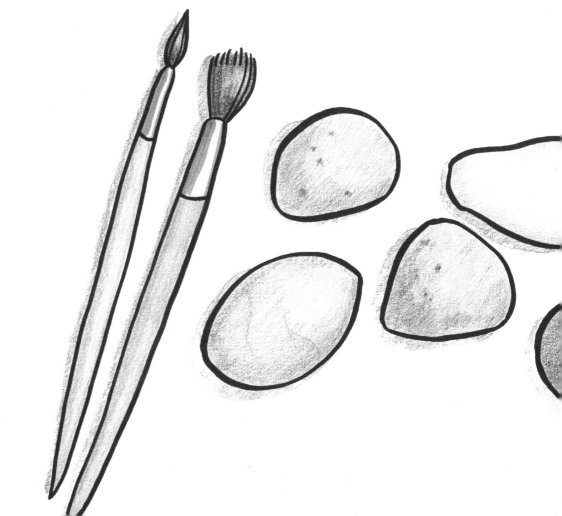

Written by Stepheni Curran
Illustrated by Samantha Williams

Meet the author and see how she is passing on the kindness!
Facebook.com/rockonkindness

Published by Orange Hat Publishing 2020

ISBN 978-1-948365-05-5
Library of Congress 2018933812

Copyrighted © 2020 by Stepheni Curran
First Edition Published in 2018
All Rights Reserved
Rock On, Kindness! Pass It On!
Second Edition
Written by Stepheni Curran
Illustrated by Samantha Williams

www.orangehatpublishing.com

I dedicate this book to my children.
May your kind and compassionate ways continue to blossom as you grow.
-S.C.

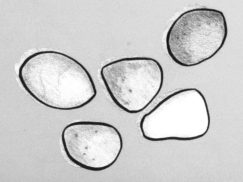

Hi!
My name is
Ally.

I am seven years old. How old are you? I am excited today for two reasons. The first reason is because I start second grade in two weeks! The second reason is because I have a **surprise** for my five best friends!

Can you predict or make a guess about what my surprise
is? I will give you a clue. My surprise

ROCKS!

So, what is your prediction?

If you predicted or guessed
my surprise has something to
do with **painted rocks**,
you are correct!

Today I am meeting my five friends at my favorite park, O'Hauser Park, to surprise them with a hunt for my painted rocks. Painted rocks? Why am I hiding painted rocks?

Well, I painted five very special rocks for my five best friends to let them know how much they mean to me. You can join in on this fun by finding the rocks I hid at O'Hauser Park.

Are you ready to hunt for my painted rocks?

Great!
Let's skip
to it!

This is my friend, Ty.

He was my first friend in my neighborhood. Ty is the oldest kid in his family, just like me. He is nine years old. He loves reading, writing, and drawing. I've been using Velcro shoes for years, but Ty said it was time for me to learn how to tie my laces, so he taught me! Now when I go to school, I'll have shoes with laces! No more Velcro for me!

Look at the five rocks I painted.

Which rock do you think I painted for Ty?

If you predicted the rock with a shoe on it, you are correct! I chose to paint the shoe green and yellow because they are Ty's favorite colors. He loves the Green Bay Packers even though he doesn't like to play football.

Instead, he likes to draw his favorite players in his sketch pad. **Do you see where I hid Ty's rock?**

Now that you know more about my friend, Ty, let me introduce you to my next friend.

Her name is **Katie.**

I met Katie when I was four years old. We were in soccer together. Katie was born without legs.

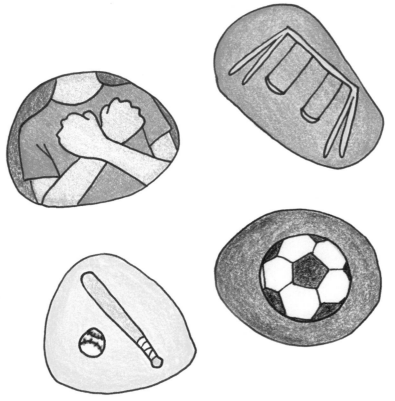

How does she play soccer? Well, she wears special equipment so she can play soccer and all sorts of sports. Katie wants to be a soccer star someday, and I really think she will be. **Which rock do you think I painted for Katie?**

If you predicted the rock with a soccer ball on it, you are on a roll! I painted a soccer ball for my friend Katie because she loves soccer. She might not have been born with legs, but her special equipment works just like legs.

I believe nothing can stop Katie. She will definitely be a soccer star someday! **Do you see where Katie's rock is hidden?**

I have told you about my friends, Ty and Katie, but I have three more friends to tell you about. That means you also have three more painted rocks to find!

My third friend is Noah.

I met Noah in swimming lessons last summer at our YMCA. Noah doesn't talk the way most of my friends talk. Noah uses a special language to talk called sign language. No, he doesn't use signs, like stop signs, to talk to me. He uses his hands to talk to me. Noah is deaf. He does not hear sounds very well. Noah is teaching me how to sign so we can talk using our hands. Just like learning any other language, this is going to take practice. I want to be able to talk to Noah, so I am going to keep learning and practicing new signs with Noah and my mom.

Look, I can already sign my name, A-l-l-y. How cool is that?

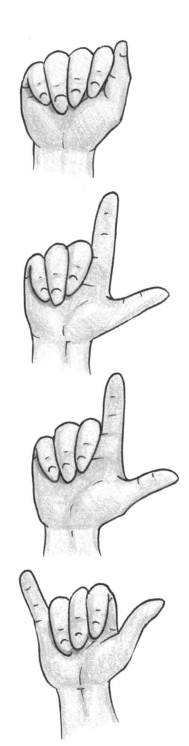

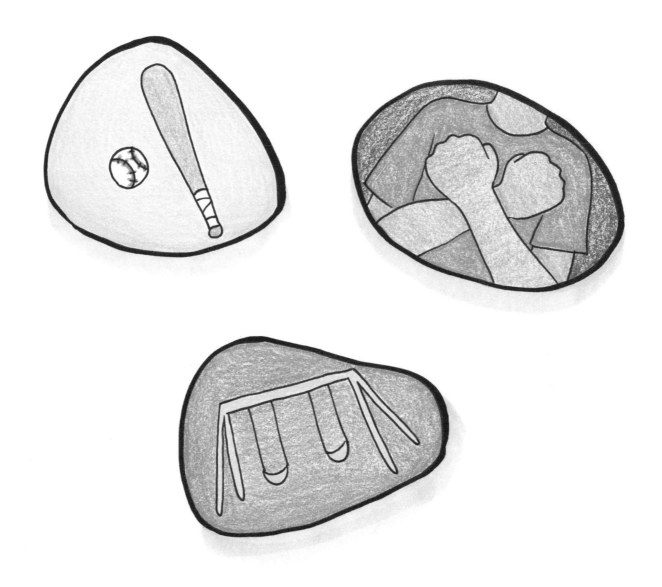

I have three painted rocks left.

Which rock do you think I painted for my friend, Noah?

If you predicted the rock with the two arms on it, you are correct! The arms show the sign for 'love' in sign language. You are so good at making predictions!

**Can you find the rock
I painted for Noah?**

on to my fourth friend named **Latifa.**

She is 7 years old just like me. Latifa lives in my neighborhood next to my friend, Ty. Latifa's family moved here from Iraq when she was just a baby. Iraq is a country that is far away from the United States. Her dad is a surgeon. He works at the hospital in our town. Latifa's family dresses differently than my family. They are Muslim. My mom told me a Muslim is someone who believes in a religion called Islam. I have a different religion than Latifa. I am a Christian. I go to a Lutheran church. Latifa and I decided we might have different religions and dress differently, but that doesn't mean we can't be friends. Latifa and I both love swinging together at the park.

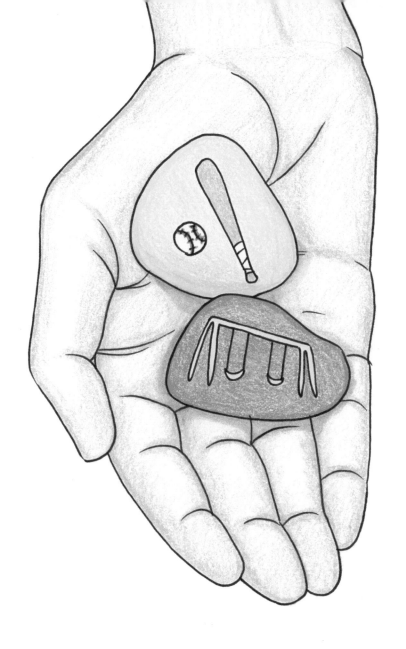

There are two rocks left.

Which rock do you predict I designed for my friend, Latifa?

If you predicted I painted a swing on the rock for Latifa, you are correct! You are so good at making predictions that you should become a meteorologist when you grow up! A meteorologist is someone who predicts the weather.

Where, oh where, did I hide Latifa's rock? Can you spot it?

I am down to my last rock for my fifth friend. His name is Max.

I met Max two months ago at a baseball game. The Milwaukee Brewers were playing against the Chicago Cubs at Miller Park. He was at the game with his family. Max is a 5 year old who loves to watch and play baseball. He also has Down syndrome. We all have tiny and important things in our bodies that make us into who we are. Max has a little extra which makes him look a bit different than me. Sometimes it takes Max longer to learn new things. Even though Max is a little different than me, we have a lot in common. We both love baseball, swimming, playing at the park, and going for walks with our dogs.

There is only one rock left, so you don't need to make a prediction. This is the rock I painted for Max. It has a baseball and a bat on it because Max loves baseball.

Where is the rock I hid for Max? Do you see it?

You did it! You found all five of the rocks I painted for my five best friends. Remember, my friends still need to find these rocks. I really want to surprise them, so please don't tell my friends where I hid these rocks.

Thanks for your help!

Ty, Katie, Noah, Latifa, and Max will be at the park very soon with their parents. Before I go, I wanted to tell you what my mom always tells me. She says,

"KINDNESS BEGINS WITH YOU!"

My friends and I are all different in our own ways. Our differences make us each unique, but our similarities make our friendships special. These painted rocks remind me of each of my friends and why I think they are so awesome! I hope these rocks make them feel happy and proud of who they are.

So ROCK ON KINDNESS, and PASS IT ON!

CPSIA information can be obtained
at www.ICGtesting.com
Printed in the USA
BVHW012109090223
658208BV00003B/199